THE BR

Peter Tinniswoo
many highly prai
them *A Touch of*
Cared, the story o
came the BBC TV
new Brandon nove atest Brigadier books,
The Brigadier Down Under and *The Brigadier in Season*,
are also available in Pan.

Also by Peter Tinniswood
in Pan Books

The Brigadier Down Under
The Brigadier in Season

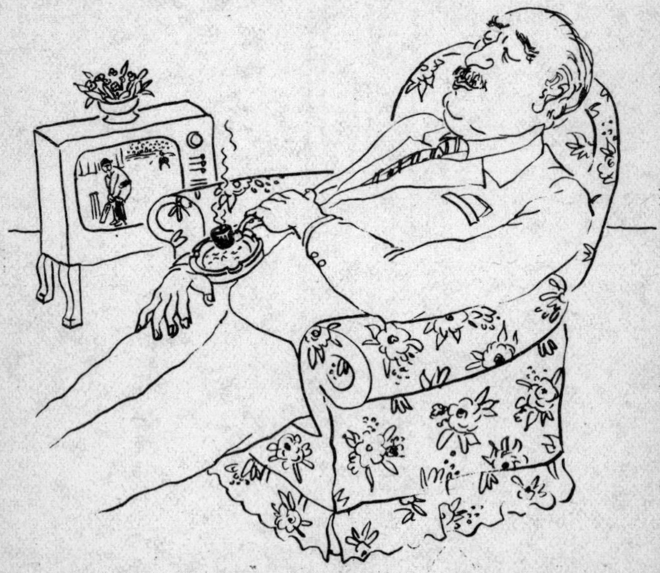

Peter Tinniswood

THE BRIGADIER'S BRIEF LIVES

Pan Original
Pan Books London and Sydney

First published 1984 by Pan Books Ltd,
Cavaye Place, London SW10 9PG
9 8 7 6 5 4 3 2 1

ISBN 0 330 28460 6

Photoset by Parker Typesetting Service, Leicester
Printed and bound in Great Britain by
Cox & Wyman Ltd, Reading

For Jim, who will understand why

MISS PETULA CLARK:

I much enjoyed watching on the moving television her series, *The History of Western Civilisation.*

I confess, though, that when she started singing with her weak little voice, I turned down the sound and played with the reamer on my pipe smoker's compendium.

It has always been a great solace to me in times of stress and hardship.

Last week I broke my dibbler while watching Lulu.

LORD CARRINGTON:

A splendid sort of cove, this.

He was, of course, elevated to the peerage for services to the Bloomsbury Set.

'Dora', among his many other accomplishments, translated Virginia Woolf into basic English, was the subject of Duncan Grant's celebrated portrait of The Nolan Sisters and was the first man to publish the works of Bloomsbury's most famous son, Mr Leslie Thomas, author of *The Virgin Solderers*.

He also acted as confidant and chief leg-waxer to E. M. Forster and taught Lord Bertrand Russell how to do difficult sums.

In later life he transferred his attentions to politics.

In that sphere he held high office for many years, being successively Under Secretary of State for Bicycle Racing, Chairman of the All Party Parliamentary Commission on Thermogene Sniffing and Minister of State for Ear Ache.

On the arrival of the Ink Monitor at Number Ten, however, he was instantly demoted to the post of Secretary of State at the Foreign Office and shortly after, with typical selflessness and moral integrity, resigned on the eve of the Combined Land, Air and Sea Task Force operation to rescue Mr Mark Thatcher from the Falkland Islands.

MR RUPERT MURDOCH:

Does he, I wonder, still live with Arthur Askey in his flat atop the BBC?

Dear old 'Stinker', how he has transformed the face of British journalism.

Since he removed the advertisements from its front page, *The Sun* newspaper has never 'looked back'.

I confess, though, I have reservations about his impact on *The Times*.

I much miss the page three pictures of William Rees-Mogg 'in the buff', the trenchant and fearless ice-hockey reports of Peregrine Worsthorne, and I feel that he was unwise in discarding the Bingo competition which so enlivened the otherwise turgid Arts Page with its dreary contributions from Michael Billington, L. Marsland Gander and Nicholas 'Ma' Jongh.

I believe he is of Australian origin.

But I do not hold that against him.

After all, he is always seen in public wearing long trousers.

Mr Richard Baker:

'Dame Janet' as he is known to his chums in the Royal Naval Reserve is without exception the finest broadcaster in the whole history of the talking wireless.

He was without shadow of doubt the finest ever chairman of *Ignorance Is Bliss*, where he tickled the fancy of the whole nation with his catchphrase, 'What a geyser'.

His inter-round summaries during the celebrated championship fight between Mr Nel Tarleton and Mr Arthur Danahar are 'classics of their kind'.

And he became a major innovator in his field when he was the first man to speak openly and frankly about cross-pollination on *Gardeners' Question Time.*

However, it is his performances on the great occasions of state that set him apart from his fellow broadcasters.

Never shall I forget the rich and moving cadences of his voice when he announced the tragic news of the engagement of Lieutenant Mark Phillips to that woman with the teeth and the sharp nose.

How one wept when he brought to the nation 'over the ether' the news of the death of the serene and beautiful Grace Archer.

How one cheered when he informed us of the official birth of Miss Mavis Nicholson.

When I die, I hope he will give the funeral oration at my graveside on his Monday morning programme on the talking wireless, even though at the time I don't suppose I shall be having a book published or issuing my latest record on the moving gramophone.

Sir John Mills:

I myself am delighted that the Ink Monitor has personally knighted him.

His mail order catalogues are an absolute 'boon' to those of who live in the country.

Unlike townies we do not have 'on our doorstep' departmental stores staffed by adenoidal, hectoring women with big things on the front of their chests and selling everything from digital toenail clippers to electronic snuff dispensers.

No, if we need to make purchases of that sort we have to engage in a major expedition to the shopping precinct at Keating New Town, and with the trusty Lanchester apparently going through 'the change of life', that can be quite a daunting experience.

And so catalogues of the sort sent out by Sir John and his surprisingly sprightly father, Hayley, are 'essential reading' for us.

I myself personally have never availed myself of the services.

But the lady wife is an avid fan, and only last week took delivery of a most reasonably priced refill for her thermal pyjamas.

Mr Ray Buckton:

In my childhood my father of late and repulsive memory was in the habit of tipping the driver of the locomotive, which drew our train from the main line junction to our beloved home station at Witney Scrotum.

The creature would doff its cap, tug its scrawny forelock and in an attitude of total subservience reminiscent of Mr Tony Lewis's behaviour in the presence of senior executives of the BBC, kiss the hem of my father's frock coat.

It lived, I believe, with its toothless mother, its sickly wife, its eighteen delinquent children and its twenty-six foul-smelling lurchers in a small terraced cottage to the rear of the open middens by Cowdrey's Bottom and 'knew its place'.

It was never heard to utter a word of complaint during the whole duration of its wretched life.

It was dedicated totally to the service of its fellow men.

Selflessly and uncomplainingly it went about its daily toil, whistling cheerfully to itself on the footplate in the vilest of weather, accepting without demur the failure of signals, the jamming of points and the terminal drunkeness of sex-crazed ticket collectors.

Its motto was simplicity itself – 'Whatever the cost, the train must get through.'

Such a man is Mr Ray Buckton.

And so is his mother, Mr Ray Illingworth.

Mr E. W. Swanton:

Without the slightest shadow of a doubt, Gloria – as he is known to his closest friends – is the finest chronicler of our beloved 'summer game' in the whole history of mankind.

I count myself fortunate indeed to be considered an intimate and chum of this truly great man.

Many are the happy hours we have spent in the garden of my home at Witney Scrotum 'yarning' about his cricketing adventures both as writer and broadcaster.

What amusing tales he has to tell of his early, formative days as a 'bobby on the beat'.

How scurrilous are his anecdotes of those years he spent as a producer of poetry among the pomaded nancy boys and rampant communists of the BBC Third Programme.

How warm and how soothing are his comments on our memories of distant heroes of the silken willow and the crimson rambler, which mellow and mature like a noble vintage wine.

And all spoken in that distinctive, rich and fruity West Country burr.

I have missed him most damnably since his retirement to Alderney.

LORD WILSON:

Formerly known as Wilson of 'The Wizard' and latterly as Sir Harold of 'Tiger Tim', I will not hear one single harsh word spoken against this tiny but perfectly formed son of the 'white rose'.

How can anyone possibly speak in an unkind manner about the only Prime Minister in the history of our dear and beloved country to have ridden six successive Grand National winners, captained his country at cricket, hockey, water polo and rugby union football, won Olympic gold medals for putting the shot, high hurdles and Graeco-Roman wrestling, single-handedly scaled Everest on no less than fourteen occasions and sailed the Atlantic in similar fashion on nineteen occasions (the last three without a boat)?

This man is a sheer colossus of multifarious talent.

He has truly been called the Des O'Connor of British politics.

As chief writer for *Coronation Street* he has delighted millions with the sensitivity of his dialogue and the acuteness of his characterisation.

And he has also given great joy and comfort in his delicate performances, acting the part of Albert Tatlock.

What a genius.

It is typical of the brilliance of the man that during his period of power he should have chosen to surround himself with people whose talents glittered and sparkled in the dull firmament of mediocrity which cloaked so many of his contemporaries.

I have it on 'good authority' that on occasions Lord

Wilson was personally acquainted with Eric Miller, Lord Kagan, Marcia Williams, Barbara Castle, HM The Queen, Sir Kenneth Lynch, Mr Matt Monro, Dennis Healey MP, Dame Vera Lynn, Herr Willy Brandt, Frau Katerina Valente, Abba, Mr William Shankley, Harold Macmillan MP, Mr Emlyn Hughes, Mr Edward Moult, Miss Louise Botting, Mr Roy Jenkins MP (but not often), David Hockney (a fellow Yorkshireman), Mrs Mary Wilson (his wife).

The height of Lord Wilson's career was reached when he was granted the supreme accolade of being invited to appear on the moving television screen in *The Morecambe and Wise Show*.

He was the one with the short, fat, hairy legs.

Mr Kevin Keegan:

Known to his friends as St Kevin, the Patron Saint of Endorsements, he is an engaging little fellow with frizzy hair and very bad grammar.

He has short bandy legs and a barrel chest and thick neck, and he makes a curious whirring noise when he runs quickly.

I think he would look rather nice on the mantelpiece next to my jar of pipe cleaners.

MR NORMAN ST JOHN STEVAS:

I well remember Norman's first visit to Witney Scrotum.

He came with a rather elderly gent who insisted on kissing our cricket pitch slightly short of a length at the hoof warehouse end and insisted that he was the Pope.

'He can't be,' I said to Norman. 'He's not a Wop.'

Norman simply smiled his saintly smile.

And blessed me thrice.

Sir Douglas Bader:

I confess I blubbed shamelessly when I learned of his death.

I never met him in person myself, but I am assured by reliable sources that he was 'a good sort'.

So, too, is Prodger Senior, our erstwhile village poacher.

Like Sir Douglas he lost both his legs in an 'accident de guerre'.

While returning from a nocturnal expedition in the copse at Cowdrey's Bottom he had the great misfortune to stumble into a Hall and Waterhouse Patent Poacher Trap.

With a hideous shriek of twanging metal its steel jaws clamped themselves round Prodger Senior's legs, of which despite their extreme bandiness and lack of hairs he had grown extremely fond.

It was a stroke of most felicitous good fortune that he was accompanied by his son, Prodger Junior, who happened to have on his person his toad skinner's scalpel.

In an instant Prodger Senior's pedicular appendages were removed from the rest of his person, and he was borne home, clutching his boots, which were later to make a most effective pair of window boxes on the front of his cottage in Ealham Alley.

What an example of fortitude he showed to all the menfolk of our village.

He repaired instantly to his bed, and there he has remained these past seventy years, pulling back the sheets only once per day, and that merely to commune with his portable umpire's commode.

How patiently he has suffered the grave inadequacies

of his wife, who seems to be quite incapable of carrying a bucket of glucose stout from our local hostelry, The Baxter Arms, to his cottage without spilling a goodly half down the front of her moleskin pinnie.

Never a word of complaint have I heard him utter against her incompetence with pipe cleaner and hedgehog reamer, her clumsiness with snuff-dispenser and betting slip and her rank idleness in changing his sou'wester and surgical smoking vest.

He is an example and inspiration to us all.

It is my firm opinion that at some time in the past he must have met Sir Douglas Bader.

Or could it have been Mr Ray Illingworth?

Mr Roy Jenkins:

I'll keep a welcome in the hillsides any day of the week for dear old 'Taffy' Jenkins.

What a tragedy that such a brilliant man should have been so cruelly cut down in his prime and in his pomp.

But then that is the fate of most Welshmen.

Look what happened to Mr Leslie Thomas.

Doomed to spend the rest of his life trapped in an endless succession of television chat shows and quiz games on the talking wireless.

Poor soul.

My heart bleeds for him.

As indeed it does for 'Taffy'.

What a waste.

Good God, he could have reached such dizzy heights.

With his inspirational powers of leadership and the magic of his charisma he could have become assistant secretary to the blessed Wilfred Wooller at our precious Glamorgan County Cricket Club.

With the magnificent purity of his diction and the mellifluousness of his voice he could have become Wales's answer to Richard Burton.

And listening to the timbre of his ringing tenor all one can say is:

'Move over, Shirley "Hogan Kid" Bassey.'

Poor old 'Taffy'.

In what desperate straits he now finds himself.

When I last saw him, I confess my heart turned over and tears coursed down my cheeks.

He was sitting in the back room of the Old Arcade

public house in Cardiff, hunched forlornly over his pint of Brains Dark, which dribbled down the front of his grubby white silk muffler and formed turgid pools on the toe caps of his industrial boots.

He looked up at me.

He fingered the blue miner's scars on the bridge of his nose, and he croaked most piteously:

'Spare us half a dollar, guv, for a glass of claret.'

SIR ROBIN DAY:

I once met Sir Robin Day in the first-class compartment of a train travelling from Salisbury to London by way of Overton, Whitchurch, Grately, Andover, Basingstoke and Woking.

He was politeness personified.

He offered me a drink of tea from the lid of his billy can.

He offered me a cheese and onion sandwich from what, if memory serves me correctly, he called his 'snap'.

When we reached Waterloo, he carried my trunk on his shoulders to the moving hackney carriage, and when I tipped him a florin piece, doffed his cap and growled warmly:

'Gawd bless you, guv. You're a proper toff.'

I wonder where he got the money from to travel first class?

MISS JAN LEEMING:

Delicious.

Delectable.

Utterly, totally, overwhelmingly desirable.

If ever a woman deserved to be a chap, it is the bewitching Jan Leeming.

PRINCE PHILIP:

I really am getting tired of this silly old Greek.

Let's face it – he's past it, isn't he?

Why doesn't he step down graciously and let someone else take over the role?

There are plenty of precedents.

Good God, *The Mousetrap* has had umpteen changes of cast.

And I've lost count of the number of different Dan Archers we've had on the talking wireless.

You see, dear readers, there comes a time in every man's life, great or humble, when it is simply 'not on' to walk around in public dressed up as an Admiral of the Fleet.

It makes a chap look a thorough-going chump.

And in these troubled times that is the last thing we want, is it not?

It crucially lowers Britain's standing in the world, if the consort of our beloved Queen is known universally as an out-and-out chump.

Could any decent, upright, typically lantern-jawed, clean-living Englishman bear the prospect of a state visit to Germany, and the President of those vile, bullet-headed, heel-clicking Huns, standing on the doorstep of his foul, sausage-stinking official residence as the royal limousine draws up, and saying out of the corner of his mouth to his obese, piggy-eyed, pink-fleshed, typically fat-necked Boche lady wife:

'Also, Liebchen, die Koenigin von England ist angekommen und . . . ach, stein mich und kleine Fischen, sie hat den alten griechischen Chump mitgebracht.'

I am not a prejudiced man, but it makes my blood boil just to think of it.

And what if the vile, garlic-munching Frogs got into the act?

What about the spaghetti-bashers from Wopland, the shoplifters from Dagoland and the frizzy-haired, thick-lipped fraternity from Niggerland who walk round dressed like deck chairs?

My God, the prospect is totally ghastly.

The man should step down instantly.

Dear Lord, this country is full of first-rate actors of 'a certain age' who would be only too willing to take on the part.

I think immediately of Mr. George Cole.

He would make a splendid job of it.

I can just imagine him standing up before the assembled peers and members of Parliament on that most noble of state occasions and saying:

'Ladies and gents,

'I am here to open Parliament on my tod, owing to the simple fact that due to a cold in the hooter Her Indoors can't be here.

'I thank you.'

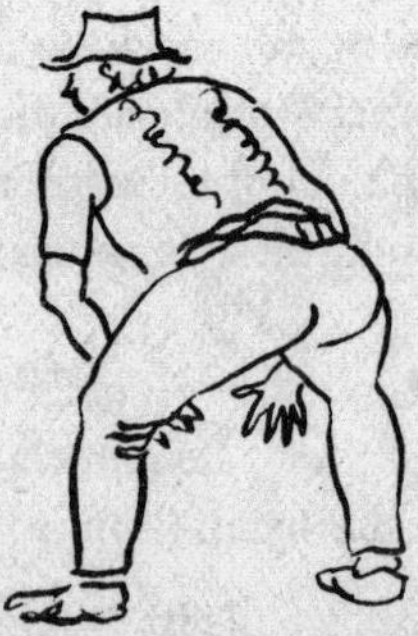

Mr Andrew Lloyd-webber:

I detest people with double-barrelled surnames.

This odious little creature and his revolting cello are no exception.

He wrote a musical about some woman who was married to the president of Argentina.

I ask you.

What's wrong with the women of this country?

Why go all the way to Argentina to rake up out of obscurity some unknown dago mobster's moll?

What about raking up the Ink Monitor at Number Ten?

'Don't cry for me, Denis Thatcher.'

LORD GOODMAN:

Like most of my fellow villagers in Witney Scrotum I am at a loss to understand why anyone in his or her right mind should elevate to the peerage an orangutan.

Yes, indeed, the world is a woeful place.

Miss Jilly Cooper:

I do like women with gaps in their front teeth.

They are so damnably useful when it comes to scraping carrots.

THE DUKE OF WESTMINSTER:

Personally, to my knowledge, I have never met 'Nat' Westminster 'in the flesh'.

However, I am prepared to concede that others probably have.

The lady wife and I were watching a programmme on the moving television recently, and she remarked:

'What that little pip needs is a good hard kick in the pills.'

I have never heard her use that word before.

I wonder if she knows what it means?

I must ask her next time I speak to her.

Mr David Frost:

The lady wife once saw him taking tea in the Ritz.

She said his table manners were impeccable, his handkerchief was spotless and he tipped most generously.

Could anyone hope for a finer epitaph?

Mr Laurie McMenemy:

He is the latest in the long and honourable line of 'pundits' who have graced our talking wireless and moving television screens over the decades.

His distinguished predecessors include Commander Campbell, Doctor C. E. M. Joad (of *Radio Fun* fame), Jacob Bronowski, Sir Julian Huxley, Gwyn Thomas (of most blessed memory), Lord David Cecil, Sir Kenneth Clark, Bernard Previn, Sir Huw Weldon, Melvyn Bragg, Dr Charles Hill, Professor Alan Gemmell, Clay Jones (the Richard Burton of horticulture), Reichsmarschall Ronald Von Pickering, David Attenborough, Jacquie Cousteau, Armand and Michaela Dennis, Hans and Lotte Hass, Professor Daniel Maskell, Dame Peter West, Dr David Bellamy, the Dowager Lady Louise Botting, Lord Desmond Wilcox, John Julius Northwich, Sir Mortimer Wheeler and his son, Jimmy, Professor Thomas Bodkin (remember how he broke that vase?), Lord Bertrand Russell and his daughter, Jane, and Mr Tony de Angeli (if that's how you spell it).

Mr McMenemy is the intellectual equal of them all, although I doubt if he is as good a footballer.

THE VILLAGE TEA LADY:

What would the village cricket teams of our noble, blessed and beloved country do without their tea ladies?

What would Witney Scrotum do without Maude Fishlock Strudwick, our very own village tea lady?

She was born in the small Sussex watering-place of Langridge-on-Sea on July 13th 1922.

She weighed seven pounds three ounces.

Her mother weighed eight stone eleven ounces.

She was the eldest of three sisters, but at the time of her birth was an only child, which seemed to affect her greatly in later life.

Her father worked in the local catarrh pastille factory until 'his accident' with a nasal inhaler on November 11th, 1929.

She attended the local Dexter Street primary school, where she was known as 'a good girl'.

She was obliged to cease formal, full-time education on the occasion of her mother's 'accident' on May 18th, 1932.

The driver of the horse-drawn heavy roller and sight-screen transporter was successfully prosecuted and convicted.

And thus did Maude Fishlock Strudwick go 'into service' with the Uftons of Ealham Abbey on December 21st, 1932.

She was known as 'a good girl'.

On the outbreak of 'hostilities' against Nazi Germany at 11 a.m., September 3rd, 1939, she left the employ of the Uftons of Ealham Abbey and joined the Army Mobile

Pigeon Service.

She served throughout the whole duration of the war, was much respected by colleagues and pigeons alike and was known as 'a good girl'.

Five weeks after the surrender of German forces at Luneburg Heath on May 4th, 1945, she returned to Langridge-on-Sea, where she took up employ as trainee invisible mender in the fretwork factory.

It was there that she met the chief balsawood buyer, Vernon Nansen Strudwick.

Their courtship lasted four years and for the whole of this period she was known as 'a good girl'.

They married at 12.33 p.m., August 8th, 1949, in the parish church of St Doggart Without Pads.

Three weeks later they moved to Witney Scrotum, where her husband took up employ as janitor in the golfball museum.

He worked there diligently until 'his accident' on September 26th, 1967.

Since that date Maude Fishlock Strudwick has devoted herself selflessly to the services of our village cricket team, where she is known as 'a good girl'.

Personally I find her pilchard sandwiches absolutely repulsive.

MISS ESTHER RANTZEN:

A person who dresses in curious frocks on the moving television and has been known to bare 'her things' from time to time.

I don't see the point.

Why women have to have them in the first place is quite beyond my comprehension.

The Ink Monitor at Number Ten hasn't got them.

But then, perhaps, she has other appendages, of which we are not aware.

ANDREW PREVIN:

Andrew has a rather curious accent, which I suspect could well be American.

If this is indeed the case, 'the authorities' should be informed immediately.

It is nothing short of scandalous that a foreigner should be allowed to 'wield the baton' in front of our great and noble English orchestras.

No wonder the Proms are jammed full of music written by Huns, Frogs and Wops.

And what are all those Irishmen doing on the talking wireless?

Terry Wogan, Frank Delaney, Henry Hunnaford, Gloria Kelly?

Trash, every man-jack of them.

I am not a prejudiced man, but if I had my way, I should turf all foreigners out of the country, confiscate their property and give them a sound and thorough thrashing with a Duncan Fearnley cricket bat.

And, talking of foreigners, where on earth does Max Jaffa come from?

I am not a prejudiced man, but I make it a firm policy never to trust anyone called Max.

I am not too happy about Rex, Leon or Sonny either.

And as for Semprini – hasn't he got a christian name?

Victor Sylvester had.

He wasn't known as 'Sylvester'.

Neither was Jack Payne.

Geraldo – there was another foreigner who was too bloody lazy to use his christian name.

Oh for the days of Henry Hall, Charlie Shadwell and Reg Leopold.

Yes, my friends, it is time for us to make a stand.

Something must be done with Andrew.

And the same goes for his odious brother, that so-called 'personality' of the moving television screen, Bernard Previn.

I am not a prejudiced man, but . . .

LORD LICHFIELD:

One-time Margate beach photographer who has 'come good'.

Ennobled in Sir Harold Wilson's retirement honours list, he has 'never looked back' since being taken up by royalty and Dame Clive James, Superstar.

He makes a fairly decent living taking snaps of young females who bare 'their things' in public, and he also advertises raincoats, check mufflers and Japanese instant cameras.

The greasy quiff of his Margate days has long since vanished to have been replaced by what seems to be a blond wig which apparently has been manufactured from an ill-fitting tea cosy.

He has also learned to sound his aitches and not slurp when drinking his soup.

To the general public he is best known for his snaps of the Royal Family.

Some measure of his success 'in that field' may be gleaned from the fact that from time to time he has managed to make Princess Anne appear vaguely human.

I must get him to take a snap of the lady wife.

Mr Geoffrey Boycott:

One of the few men whose name has become part of the standard vocabulary of the English language.

I quote from the dictionary:

'To geoff – to refuse to hold relations of any kind with a colleague so as either to punish him or coerce him into abandoning his position (e.g. "He geoffed me so many times I was forced to leave Yorkshire" – John Hampshire).

'In cricket parlance also means to run out or play golf in India.'

Mrs Mary Whitehouse:

She is the sort of woman any man would be proud to call 'mother' (or even 'father', if he were hard pressed) and has never been known to bare 'her things' in public.

Over the years she has crusaded fearlessly and diligently to rid this country of the vileness and filth which has threatened to swamp it in a torrent of ghastliness and a flood of sheer and utter frightfulness.

She has campaigned with outstanding success against some of the foulest excesses committed in the name of 'good art'.

She herself was personally responsible for the defenestration of Boy George.

By her efforts and her efforts alone were the rampantly erotic paintings of Sir Peter Scott banished from public view.

On her initiative and her initiative alone was every mention of titty deleted from the works of Mr Arthur Ransome.

But most notable of all was the occasion when she 'took on' the scum who run the National Theatre and accused them before judge and jury of putting on a production that was an open encouragement and incitement to the masses to commit outbreaks of sodomy, masturbation, men dressing up in their lady wives' togs, bed wetting, nude bicycling, acts of nose picking in public, armpit sniffing between consenting adults, bestiality with Bedlington Terriers and members of the Household Cavalry, doing rude things with tightly rolled-up copies of *The Cricketer*, going to bed without pyjamas, wearing aftershave lotion, farting in the bath and failing to shake one's Thing properly after visiting the ablutions offices.

Scandalously and infamously, the judge threw out her case lock, stock and barrel.

And, shamelessly, the production of *Dear Octopus* was allowed to continue unhindered.

SIR RICHARD ATTENBOROUGH:

How well I remember his stunning performance as Pinky and Perky in *Brighton Rock.*

How vividly I recall the chubbiness of his kneecaps in *The Wilmslow Boy*.

He is indisputably one of the all-time greats of the moving kinomatographic screen.

'Duke', as he is known to his myriad fans in all corners of the globe, has a range of acting ability which in my opinion can only be bettered by his friend and mentor, the sublime and subtle Sir Donald Sinden, who recently and most deservedly was awarded his knighthood for services to the nation's elocution teachers.

And what joy Sir Richard has brought to his legions of admirers with those distinctive catchphrases of his, which have so indelibly engraved themselves into our country's cultural heritage:

'Can I do you now, sir?'

'You're an absolute shower.'

'Hello, campers.'

Here in Witney Scrotum we celebrate his birthday annually with fireworks and ox-roasting even though he is a short-arsed twerp with a profoundly irritating lisp.

Mr Robert Robinson:

He is celebrated the length and breadth of this country and its attendant isles and possessions overseas as the chap on the moving television screen who stretches his hair like trip-wires over his bald patches.

I wonder why people do that.

I must ask the lady wife's spinster sister next time she comes to visit us at Witney Scrotum.

Yes, he's a real 'chip off the old block', is he not?

Brave to the point of foolhardiness, a brilliant orator, a rapier-sharp debater, dashing, handsome, debonaire, gallant, witty, incurably romantic – no wonder the Ink Monitor at Number Ten is besotted by him.

And what a lovely couple they make.

I myself came across them while they were making a secret tour by tandem of Northern France.

They cycled past by our trusty Lanchester, smiling happily, gazing into each other's eyes and holding hands – which probably explains why they fell arse over tit at the next roundabout.

LORD LONGFORD:

A doddery old cove with a bald head and damp teeth.

He is the father of the sublime and virtuous Lady Antonia Frazier and her brother, Joe, the former heavy-weight champion of the world.

He is the sort of person who eats bits off the dog's basket and says:

'I say. These are awfully good pretzels.'

He is a notable champion of 'lost causes' as evinced by his constant efforts to be taken seriously.

I confess I blubbed shamelessly when he 'fell from grace' with such tragic and brutal swiftness.

In my opinion, if men in public life wish to conduct clandestine relationships with women with big things on the front of their chests, that is their business and their business alone.

Only the prurient and the incurably nosey would think otherwise.

Unfortunately scum of this sort, along with slack-jawed, concave-shinned Northerners, form the vast majority of the population of this dear country of ours, and thus was this near-saintly man pilloried, humiliated and finally destroyed.

Pity him, dear readers, in his long and barren exile Down Under.

Only one thing consoles me.

It is this:

He still retains the love, affection and loyalty of his dear lady wife, Mary Poppins Parkinson, who, despite the hardships and deprivations of her life, still manages to send him the occasional food parcel and mohair suit from time to time.

For myself I have only one thing to say:

'Come back, Parky.

'This country still needs you.

'And so do the Ink Monitor at Number Ten and the makers of Brylcreem.'

Mr Terry Wogan:

I suppose I had better mention him in my book.
    If I don't, he will.

MR DAVID ATTENBOROUGH:

It is said by the so-called experts with their limp bow ties and nancy-boy girlfriends that this near-saintly man has opened up new vistas and horizons of comprehension for the ignorant scum who form the vast majority of the audience who spend their evenings in front of the moving television screen, picking their noses, belching and sniffing the insides of their surgical slippers.

The gory disembowelment of wildebeest by ravenous lions.

The public and shameless copulation of giant turtle and New Forest pony.

The mutual smelling of private parts by Arctic fox and Australian dingo.

The gobbling up of its mate by female praying mantis.

These they cite as examples of 'the windows of the world' opened up to the slack-jawed masses with their bad teeth, dandruff and endemic smoker's coughs.

Stuff and nonsense.

The trash have only to open the front doors of their wall-to-wall carpeted, home-computered, videoed, tumble-dried hovels and step into the streets to see infinitely more ghastly visions of Mother Nature 'in the raw'.

Worse still, they could be compelled to take a look inside the dressing room of the Yorkshire County Cricket Club.

MR ROY PLOMLEY:

This dear, saintly man is quite rightly known throughout the civilised world as the Queen Mother of British broadcasting.

Hasn't he got a lovely voice for speaking?

How I love his programme on the talking wireless.

I wonder which eight records I should chose to take with me.

Well, I should certainly take this one:

'Most catches taken in the field in a first class cricket match in India . . . six by L. M. Deas, Europeans versus Parsees, Poona, 1889.'

And I should take this one, too:

'Most aitches dropped in a day in a BBC ball-by-ball radio commentary . . . 97 by F. S. Trueman, England versus Australia, Lords, 1977.'

As for the rest, well, I should let Roy make the choice, for he is obviously a man of such towering good taste, wisdom and culture.

Dear Roy, is it not amazing that one man can have so many dear, close and personal friends?

You see, dear readers, it is a fact not generally known that every single person who appears on *Desert Island Discs* is a close and personal friend of Roy.

Oh yes.

You won't get on his programme just because you've got a book coming out, or you're appearing in a play that's doing badly in the West End or you're directing that latest American musical about to open at the National Theatre.

Oh no.

Roy 'isn't like that'.

That emaciated vileness, Tinniswood, once tried to worm his way on the programme and, I can tell you, he was sent packing with 'a flea in his ear'.

Mr Sebastian Coe:

A young man of sallow complexion, who appears to have the ambition to run faster than anyone else in the world.

With a personality like his I think he is very wise.

MISS PAMELA STEPHENSON:

An Australian person who once bared 'her things' from time to time on the moving television.

I don't see the point myself.

Why women have to have them in the first place is quite beyond my comprehension.

They don't have them in Witney Scrotum.

And neither has Miss Jan Leeming.

And look what a splendid chap she is.

Mr Arthur Scargill:

Do not be alarmed, dear readers.

He is perfectly harmless.

My father of foul and deadly memory once had a native bearer just like him.

Every morning he would take down his pants and thrash him mercilessly on his native dusky buttocks with the handle of his portable Gunn and Moore cricket bat until the gore ran like billy-o.

And the brute worshipped him.

It is exactly the same with trade union leaders.

They like the rough stuff.

Treat them like contemptible scum, and you'll have them eating out of your hands.

Debase them, abuse them, defile them, humiliate them, and they'll do anything for you.

How else do you imagine Scargill got anyone to give him that silly haircut?

Mr Roy Hattersley:

It is said he is to be the model for the next pavilion at Bramall Lane.

He is best known as a frequent contributor to the Country Diary column of the incomparable *Manchester Guardian.*

He is a plump, fresh-faced young man, who looks well in khaki shorts and stout walking shoes.

He is, in fact, Shadow Minister for Hiking in the House of Commons.

His first hiking exploits occurred in his native Sheffield, where he was known to plod the bleak fastness of The Moor, reciting out loud to the incomprehending sheep and Irish drunks the words of his beloved St Raymond D'Illingworth, and later in the evening he would slake his thirst in the crystal-clear waters of Barker's Pool and dream strong dreams of distant hikes carrying on his head the baggage for Yorkshire County Cricket Club.

He has indeed hiked far and wide since those early days.

It might explain why he is always out of breath when he appears on the moving television screen.

Mr Ian Paisley:

I have in my possession the following report written 'some time ago' by a commanding officer.

It reads thus:

'The sarn't major has an extremely loud voice.

'His neck glows red, when he shouts, and his eyes pop out.

'He is not popular with the men.'

I confess to being somewhat surprised by these remarks.

I have never met the man personally, but whenever I have seen him interviewed on the moving television screen, he has always been politeness personified when talking about his achievements with his beloved Liverpool Football Club.

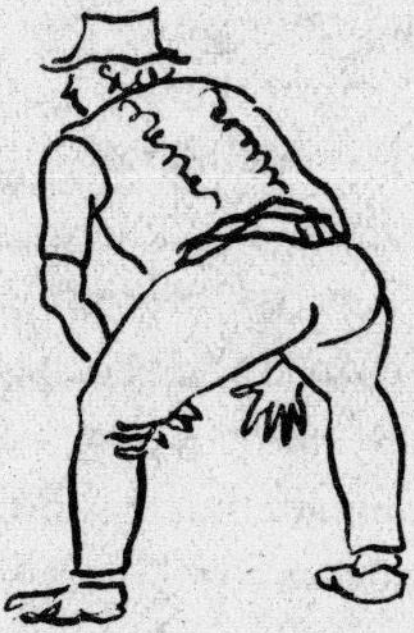

He is this country's chief 'left footer'.

As indeed he was many years ago when, known to his admirers as 'Joe', he played with such distinction for Arsenal Football Club.

I am not a prejudiced man.

I have nothing against them.

On the whole, even though they are 'out of step' with the majority of the inhabitants of this country, they are honest, upright and decent citizens.

They have a certain arrogance, it is true.

They consider themselves to be exclusive.

They always maintain that they are 'in the right'.

They have a tendency to feel persecuted, particularly in the industrial heartlands of the North of England.

But in the main they have contributed greatly over the years to the well-being of this blessed and beloved country of ours.

It is just that, with the exception of Mr Joe Mercer, I prefer chaps who play for Tottenham Hotspur.

MR IAN BOTHAM:

It is said that the Ink Monitor at Number Ten was moved to tears when Mr Ian Botham, the Dennis Skinner of first class cricket, single-handedly won the Ashes for England in the summer of '81.

It is said, too, that His Holiness the Pope, on hearing the news of Mr Botham's blistering double century against the Indian tourists of '82, instantly ordered all the great man's literary works to be fetched from the Vatican library and spent the rest of the evening practising his off-drive in front of his stripped-pine wardrobe mirror.

It is said that Mr Botham's vicious dismemberment of the New Zealanders of '83 prompted our glorious and beautiful Queen to offer him forthwith command of the Task Force she had assembled to subdue the rebels of Yorkshire County Cricket Club, to refurbish and refortify the pavilion at Bramall Lane and patrol in force the massive earthworks of Sellers' Dyke.

This may well have been the case, but those exploits had absolutely no effect whatsoever on the lady wife.

Typical.

Nothing impresses her.

If she were to be granted the greatest honour known to mankind, a personal audience of Mr E. R. 'Elizabeth Regina' Dexter, I know what she would say.

'Hasn't he got a big nose?' she would say.

Typical.

She should talk, anyway.

MR MICHAEL FOOT:

He had a brother called Dingle.

Nice name, Dingle.

Dingle, Dingle, Dingle.

It ripples and tinkles over the tongue, does it not?

In my opinion it is a christian name which should have been employed more frequently among our public figures.

Prince Dingle of Wales.

Sir Dingle Boycott.

Dingle J. Kramer and the Dakotas.

Pope Dingle the Second.

Mr Dingle Du Cann.

Boy Dingle.

Dingle . . .

What the devil was I talking about?

Ah yes – Michael Foot.

Nice chap.

What a pity he wasn't called Dingle.

MR H. D. 'DICKY' BIRD:

I passed by 'Dicky' quite recently on a glum and gloomy afternoon at Lords.

He was sitting on his portable umpire's commode.

He had a contented smile on his face.

And he was singing softly to himself the following Fred Astaire song:

'I'm putting on my flat cap,
'Taking out my meter,
'And offering the light.'

His voice had a surprisingly gentle and lilting contralto quality.

Mr Frank Muir:

An extremely tall man who sniffs a lot and wears pink bow ties.

Personally I find bow ties of any sort utterly abhorrent.

What a thoroughly pleasant old stick.

I just so wish his beautiful daughter hadn't married that booby with the bald patch and the sticky-out ears.

Surely to goodness she could have done better for herself?

I know for a fact that Mike Brearley was available at the time.

And so were Roy Hattersley and Mr H. D. 'Dicky' Bird.

What a wonderful wife she would have made for dear old 'Dicky'.

And what an asset to him.

Just think of the burdens she could have taken off his stooped old shoulders.

She could have polished his little light meter, ironed the peak of his flat cap, oiled the lid of his snap tin, gone walk-around in his stead at Headingley and Burton-on-Trent.

What a waste.

Mind you, her father has had his ups and downs, hasn't he?

He's got that wife who always seems to have lipstick on her teeth.

And, worst of all, he's got that mother-in-law.

I think it is thoroughly wretched the way life displays such rottenness towards the more amiable members of the human race.

Just look at the plight of poor Captain Mark Phillips.

Mr Jimmy Hill:

He is the son of the famous and much-loved Dr Charles Hill, known in a previous life as 'The Radio Doctor'.

Jimmy has followed in his father's footsteps and is now known to millions as 'The Television Quack'.

He learned English at an early age while serving as auxiliary ablutions wallah to Scottish Highland troops stationed in Port Said.

Later with his elder brother he stowed away on the bulk night-soil carrier HMS *Repulse* and entered this country as an immigrant at Southampton in the early fifties.

At first he and his brother earned a somewhat precarious living in the music halls where they were known as 'Leon Cortez and Doreen'.

But soon with commendable enterprise and industry he secured the exclusive British franchise for the marketing of Colonel Ghadafi's Fried Kentucky Piles Ointment.

From that moment he 'never looked back'.

He settled himself in some luxury in an elegant country house in Bradenham in the county of Buckinghamshire.

He acquired a town house in London and there, fêted by society and lionised by his peers, he decided to enter politics.

Three times he fought the seat of High Wycombe and lost.

But finally, after defeat at Taunton, he was elected Conservative Member of Parliament for Maidstone.

His maiden speech in the House was a total and abject failure and led to his speaking those memorable lines:

'I will sit down now, but the time will come when you will hear me.'

By God, how right he was.

Look where he is now.

MR JIMMY SAVILLE OBE:

Well, he bloody well didn't fix it for me.

I rang him and said:

'Look here, the plug's gone on the Hoover again.'

And what happened?

Nothing.

The lady wife and I waited in for him for six days running, and there wasn't a squeak from him.

Then we switched on the moving television set, and there he was running in some blasted marathon race.

Typical of the modern British workman.

MISS ELIZABETH JANE HOWARD:

People always remember chaps who use both their christian names.

I remember a batman I once had in the Sudan.

His name was 'Petey Brian', and he was a thief, a liar and a nancy-boy to boot.

My mother once had a chambermaid called 'Marigold May', and she used to suck dried peas.

Revolting habit.

I expect Elizabeth Jane Howard does it, too.

For what other reason could she and Mr Denis Amiss have divorced?

MR TONY BENN:

A very shuperior short of Shoshialisht.

MR TOM STOPPARD:

He is the husband of the celebrated personality of the moving television screen, Dr Rod Buckman, and a distinguished playwright 'in his own right'.

He has had 'versions' of his plays performed all over the world.

Arthur Miller's adaptation and translation of *Jumpers* was an outstanding success in New York.

The Pam Gems version of the Ionesco translation of the David Hare adaptation of the Schnitzler 'free transcription' of *Rosencrantz is Dead* also did quite well.

He is currently at work adapting *Wisden Cricketers' Almanack* for the National Theatre's first British musical.

MR BOB WILLIS:

He is best known perhaps as the creator of *Dixon of Dock Green* on the moving television screen.

He is also the tallest man ever to have captained England at cricket.

I like records, don't you?

See if you know the answers to the following questions.

Which captain of England had:

1. The smallest feet?
2. The ugliest wife?
3. The vilest temper?
4. The wiriest pubic hair?
5. The smelliest socks?
6. The highest singing voice?
7. The greatest number of interviews with Mr David Frith?
8. The greatest number of moles on his back?
9. The greatest number of catches in a single innings?
10. The most praise from Doctor Frederick Trueman, Bramall Lane Emeritus Professor of Dropped Aitches and Difficult Sums?

Answers, please, to Mr Ian Sproat, who will be editor of next year's *Cricketers' Who's Who*, if the players are idiots enough to fill in his questionnaires without demanding a share of his royalties.

Mr Barry Took:

Mr Barry Took is rightly known as 'the father of British comedy'.

Such is his innate modesty and painful shyness that only the smallest handful of people know that he was the only begetter and creator of *Monty Python's Flying Circus.*

'Tell you what, Lofty,' he once said. 'If you want to get anywhere, you want to start walking funny.'

This Mr John Cleese did, and he has never looked back since – save to make sure he is not being followed by Mr Barry Took.

Miss Britt Ekland:

A person of mature years who has been known to bare 'her things' from time to time on the talking kinematographic screen.

I don't see the point.

Why women have to have them in the first place is quite beyond my comprehension.

Maybe her father, the celebrated jockey, Mr Edgar Britt, knows the answer.

But then I don't suppose he does.

He is a much nicer person than his daughter.

And his legs are shapelier, too.

BRITT

SIR PETER HALL:

The first Chinaman to be appointed director of the National Theatre.

He is also chairman of the Kowloon Steam Tiepin Company, deputy chairman of the Taiwan Disposable Wellington Boot Corporation and is on the board of the Barbican Share-A-Flat Service and The League of the Friends of Harold Pinter.

He lists his hobbies as 'taking long walks in Norfolk and going to the National Theatre'.

Sir Geoffrey Howe:

I have it on 'good authority' that the remark most frequently passed in the House of Commons these days is this:

'Don't ask Howe – ask Why.'

Sie Geoffrey is the sort of person who never cleans his spectacles until he starts walking into lamp posts.

He bumps his head a lot, too, and finds difficulty in tying his boot laces.

The Ink Monitor is in the process of patenting his voice as an instant cure for insomnia.

In my opinion he is totally harmless.

When he and his wife visited us recently at Witney Scrotum, he occupied himself happily throwing sticks at the horse chestnut for conkers.

He got seven.

Although he twice set the cat on fire, broke three bottles of Tizer and fell asleep during the shipping forecast on the talking wireless, he was an agreeable enough guest. Especially when he was in 'the land of Nod'. Which to my admittedly untutored eyes seemed to be all the time.

Mr James Cameron:

He is editor of the *Manchester Guardian*, and, more importantly, has developed to perfection the art of talking on the moving television screen whilst sucking three bags of mint imperials and half the keyboard of a piano accordion.

He is 'a thoroughly good sort'.

I much enjoyed his *Case Book* and was always on his side in his battles against Doctor Snoddie.

Lord Lucan:

Is he dead or is he living?

Who cares?

I was never totally convinced that he was in the land of the living in the first place.

I think I saw him recently on the moving television screen sucking Mr John Aspinall's eyebrows dressed in a gorilla skin.

His biggest mistake was when he gave up playing Old Mother Riley.

MR NED SHERRIN:

He is that curious-looking cove on the moving television screen, who has a face like the inside of a Mothercare child's plastic pottie.

Those 'in the know' consider him to be 'too clever by half'.

However, my good friend Mr Caryl Brahms who has had 'dealings' with him from time to time tells me he is perfectly harmless if you give him an occasional thorough thrashing.

He is the author of *Side by Side with the Bedser Twins.*

The Archbishop of Canterbury:

It is not generally known that in his youth Bob served as curate in Witney Scrotum.

He was much loved by the congregation and his impersonation of Doctor Michael Ramsey, who managed England to victory in the World Cup of '66, was greatly admired by all.

He was unfailingly kind to old ladies, including Grannie Swanton, Don 'Sir Oswald' Mosey, and doddery old Arlott, to whom he regularly distributed Peter Dominic gift vouchers.

He was Hon. Sec. of the Witney Scrotum train spotters' club, and when he bought his first car uttered that celebrated ecumenical remark:

'I lisped in Humbers because the Humbers came.'

Personally I don't ever remember seeing him.

PRINCESS MARGARET:

A rather portly lady of mature years, related, it is said, by birth to the Royal Family.

I, however, am not convinced.

Her appearance suggests to me that she could well be the mother of Mr Leon Brittan.

Indeed, on further reflection I am led to the firm belief that she *is* Mr Leon Brittan.

Miss Jean Rook:

I count myself privileged indeed to be a founder member of the Save Jean Rook for the Nation Fund.

It would be tragic if this noble and historic edifice were to be allowed to crumble and collapse through neglect and apathy.

Institutions such as these are not permanent, dear readers.

They need constant attention.

They need vast sums of money spent on essential repairs and maintenance.

We simply cannot rely on the annual *Blue Peter* Christmas Appeal to provide the necessary funds.

All of us as patriotic Englishmen (and Englishwomen, if the cap fits) have a bounden duty to 'dip into our pockets' to ensure the preservation for posterity of this national treasure.

Mr Norman Tebbitt:

It is claimed that he is living proof of the theory that 'Archie Andrews lives on'.

I myself favour the view that he is worked by long wire rods made from metal coat hangers.

'Kermit', as he is known to his closest friends, is the creator of the official Conservative Party policy of instant disembowelment as a cure for unemployment.

He once called in on us unexpectedly at Witney Scrotum, and the lady wife gave him a sound thrashing with her bicycle pump and adaptor.

He seemed to like it.

Mr Mick Jagger:

A fanatic of our beloved 'summer game', he developed his stage technique from a close study of Mr Derek Randall's stance at the wicket.

His singing style is self-taught and is thought to be the result of formative years spent at The Oval listening to Mr Robin Jackman appealing for LBW.

He is known as 'the Alec Bedser of rock'.

Mr Patrick Moore:

With his partner, Mr Gunn, he invented the cricket bat.

He also pioneered the use of matting wickets on the surface of the moon and was the first man to place a heavy roller into orbit around Jupiter.

His theory that Meteor Crater, Arizona, is the result of the impact of cricket balls struck into outer space by Mr Ian Botham has still to be ratified by scientists of the Test and County Cricket Board.

DOCTOR DAVID OWEN:

I confess I blubbed shamelessly when he left politics and founded the SDP.

Mr Jimmy Young:

The father of the celebrated star of the moving kinematograph, Miss Loretta Young, Mr Jimmy 'Brigham' Young is an erstwhile 'crooner' who now has a programme on the talking wireless.

It consists entirely of 'Freezer Specials'.

The chief freezer is the Ink Monitor from Number Ten.

It is understood she successfully deep-froze Mr Young some three years ago.

Sir Anthony Blunt:

I confess I blubbed shamelessly when I heard the news of his death.

He was formerly By Appointment Chief Antique Dealer and Picture Restorer to Her Majesty the Queen.

He was dismissed with some ignominy when he was discovered sitting at the foot of her bed in the 'early hours' drinking Babycham.

With great presence of mind Her Majesty summoned a footman, and Sir Anthony left with him with undisguised pleasure.

MR CLIVE JENKINS:

Here at Witney Scrotum we have just been granted the supreme and ultimate accolade – Mr Clive Jenkins has purchased a property in the village.

It is the Old Rectory.

I am proud to say that I had the honour of being conducted through the house by Clive himself in person, who showed with justifiable pleasure the alterations he had made.

I was particularly struck with the murals depicting 'The Plighte and Sorrie Predicament of the Working Classes' and the moving and tragic 'Mass Exodus of the Welsh to Little Venice'.

I wish him well in his new abode.

Mr Enoch Powell:

He is one of the truly great men of his generation.

He should be an inspiration to all of us in these wretched times of dole queues, nuclear waste, urban despoilation, earthquakes, famine, wars and the records of Mary O'Hara.

His is the classic immigrant's story – the humble birth in the poverty-stricken, cruelly exploited, far-flung outpost of the Black Country, the formative years spent fighting for survival in an alien and deeply prejudiced society, which frequently showed open hostility to the strange colour of his skin, the unfamiliar cadences of his accent and the curious errors of his pronunciation, and, finally, the arrival in London, the purchase of Homburg hat and second-hand undertaker's suit and the rise to a position of power and pre-eminence second only to that enjoyed by Mr David Jacobs.

It is a story to be cherished and honoured.

Even now I thrill to the very core of my soul when I hear his noble clarion call ring out loud and clear in the corridors of power:

'Can you hear me, mother?'

Indeed we do hear.

And we cling to his every word.

He has graced the public life of our dear and beloved country with wit, grace and gentle modesty and, despite the loathsomeness of his quiff, the legacy of his early days spent in the employ of the borough of Wolverhampton as assistant municipal ballroom dancing instructor (tango division), and the repulsive appearance of his skin, which to my admittedly untutored eyes has the colour and texture of a used tea-bag and is, I suspect, the result of the long and arduous years spent on the night shift of the Burslem branch of the CWS Wholesale Dry Cleaners as deputy Hoffman presser whilst he struggled for funds to pay his way through 'varsity' and gain his diploma in 'Rudimentary English', he is indeed a credit to his 'native heath', despite the vileness of his moustache, which to my admittedly untutored eyes bears a marked resemblance to a hamster's pubic hairs.

Personally, I agree entirely with his political philosophy.

Yes, the government should instantly supply funds for the repatriation of every single Black Countryman to their revolting, tubercular-riddled hovels in the adenoidal fastness of their tribal homelands.

Mr Enoch Powell is one of nature's 'originals'.

LADY FALKLANDER:

How often in recent years has the following question been asked:

Where were you on that fateful day?

What were you doing at the very moment when single-handedly, fearlessly and boldly the Ink Monitor at Number Ten personally led the attack on the Falkland Islands?

I know what I was doing.

I was in the ablutions offices attending to an urgent call of nature.

By God, I wish I'd stayed there.

Miss Jan Morris:

Formerly famous as the mother of the celebrated Australian Test batsman, Mr Arthur Morris.

Now, after a change of lifestyle, she is better known as the father of the moving television screen animal impersonator, Mr Johnny Morris.

MR LUDOVIC KENNEDY:

He is without doubt the most famous and best-loved man in contemporary Britain.

And, my God, he seems to have been going for ages and ages, doesn't he?

He does not like to talk about it, but he is, in fact, owing to the idiosyncracies of the time warp, in the fifth manifestation of his existence.

How amazing that he is still as sprightly and lively as the day he stepped out of the Tardis all those years ago.

Mr Brian Redhead:

I do wish someone would tell him.

On and on and on, he goes.

Is it really necessary to talk quite so much?

It's that chap, John Timpson, I feel sorry for.

He's trapped.

There is nowwhere he can go.

Redhead's the sort of chap who would follow him to the ablutions offices and stand outside the door talking.

On and on and on and on.

Selina Scott wouldn't do it.

Neither would Sue Lawley.

They would wait until he came out, and then they'd start on him.

On and on and on and on.

I wonder what this Redhead creature looks like?

There is no way of knowing, of course, but I suspect he is an extremely small individual with beady eyes and a silly, unkempt beard that just about meets in the middle.

Or could that be Libby Purves?

Mr Brian Johnson:

I first met Jonners in the company of Swanners, Blowers and that emaciated vileness, Tinners, on a lovely summer day at Fenners.

'Hello, Jonners,' I said.

'Hello, Briggers,' he said.

I think he's a bit of a twerp, talking like that, don't you?

Mr Reginald Bosanquet:

I confess I blubbed shamelessly when he disappeared from our moving television screens.

In those halcyon days the news was always good, wasn't it?

No strikes, no wars, no Ink Monitor at Number Ten, just the odd earthquake or two in Dagoland and assassination attempts on Australian cricket captains.

And how he enjoyed himself.

The twinkling eyes.

The quivering lips.

The flush of excitement on his cheeks.

Not that like glum cove with the broken nose and adenoids and the other one with the pock-marked face.

Since they've taken over we have had nothing but wretched summers, royal weddings and the raising of the *Mary Rose.*

Mr Bosanquet would not have allowed this sorry state of affairs to occur.

He'd have come on the moving television screen and said:

'Here is the news.

'The price of malt whisky has been slashed.

'Pubs are going to be open all day.

'Any female found baring "her things" in public will be soundly thrashed by Lord Longford wearing nothing but fireman's helmet and string vest.

'Reginald Bosanquet.

'News At Ten.

'Baxter Arms.

'Witney Scrotum.'

Yes, indeed, he is a most grievous loss to the nation.

And, incidentally, have you noticed that if you remove the 'o' and the 's' from his name, you are left with 'banquet'.

Rather appropriate, don't you think?

Mr Auberon Waugh:

One of the finest Englishmen it has ever been my privilege to meet in person.

We encountered each other, when he came to Witney Scrotum to play cricket as skipper of the Princess Michael of Kent Select XI.

What a charming collection of 'chums' he brought with him.

The team in batting order, if memory serves me correct (and it usually doesn't), was as follows:

Sir James Goldsmith, Lord Goodman, Mr Bernard Shrimsley, Mr Harold Evans, Sir John Junor, Waugh himself with Mr Richard Inghams as runner, George Pope the Second, Prince Charles, Mr Brian Rix, Mr Larry Adler and an exceedingly small person, who said he was the editor of a cricket magazine, the name of which I forget.

I myself bowled Auberon first ball for 'a blob'.

He just smiled at me faintly.

MR BILL SOWERBUTTS:

Although I have never met him personally, I look upon him as a close and dear friend.

I feel that he would always be there, 'a shoulder to cry on', 'a tower of strength' in adversity, 'a fountain of wisdom' constant and true.

It is the voice that does it, I suppose.

It is rich and loamy.

Earthy.

Tangy.

It has a deeply masculine solidity.

Or have I mixed it up with Mavis Nicholson?

Mr Jim Laker:

What a smashin' man.
His battin' wasn't as good as Gattin'.
But his bowlin' was better than Parkin.

Mr Jackie Stewart:

An amazingly ugly Scottish midget with a voice like a defective exhaust pipe.

The lady wife proffers the opinion that he is an escapee from a book by Tolkien.

Miss Roebuck from the dog biscuit shop is convinced that he is a previously unknown species of tropical parrot.

I myself believe that he is just 'one of those things' that unfortunately happen from time to time.

LORD KAGAN:

I once bought one of his macs and first time on the blasted thing got ripped to shreds in the chain guard of the lady wife's bicycle.

Bloody foreigners!

SIR HAROLD MACMILLAN:

He is the father of the tennis doubles player who wears that absurd white peaked hat and used to play with that bearded bald-headed lout who became South African after having been Australian, and serve the bugger right.

Personally I find all professional tennis players totally detestable.

Curiously enough I have no such feelings about speedway riders.

Dear old 'Split' Waterman – whatever became of him?

MR JOHN WELLS:

I first met dear 'Bomber' during the early days of the last war, when he came to our village of Witney Scrotum as an evacuee.

What a pathetic little figure he was.

Pinched and sallow cheeks, pointed and flapping ears, spindly legs, hollow chest, threadbare baggy trousers, ill-fitting boots with no laces and all permeated by the ghastly adenoidal whine of his native Walsall – poor little chap, he hardly knew the difference between litotes and metalepsis and had, I swear, never before set eyes on a genuine fin-de-siècle Sevres moustache warmer.

The lady wife took an instant 'shine' to him, and it was not long before she had released him from the vile clutches of the tyrannical old Squire Brearley who had been sending the poor wretch up his chimneys to remove the soot and the remnants of charred cricket bags.

Consequently when poor 'Bomber' arrived at our home, he looked for all the world like an emaciated and shrunken Mr V. S. Naipaul, though, I am bound to say, his writing was of a vastly superior quality.

The lady wife was quick to 'dose him up' with copious supplies of Virol, halibut oil capsules, gregory powder and hound conditioner, and in next to no time she had 'licked him into shape'.

I myself saw little of him at this time owing to the fact that I had forbidden him to live in the house.

I couldn't stand his hairs all over the cushions and five minutes in his company was sufficient to cause my eyes to water most frightfully and to bring up a scarlet rash on the front of my shins.

Thus the lady wife set up quarters for him in some disused outbuildings at the bottom of the garden.

She treated him well.

He was taken for exercise five times per day.

He was wormed at regular intervals.

And he was taught to rattle the window latch with his nose, when he wanted to attract attention.

Attention he did indeed attract, for 'in next to no time' he proved himself to be a creature of the most formidable intellectual qualities.

In one of the outbuildings placed at his disposal there were trunkfuls of old books long since discarded by the lady wife in the interests of 'space'.

Dear old 'H.G.' (as we now called him) discovered this 'hoard' and soon immersed himself in them, pillaging and feasting on the treasures contained therein.

Imagine our astonishment when we discovered that having read these dusty volumes 'Dee' (as we affectionately designated him) was conversant with the whole cannon of ancient Greek literature, could recite 'off by heart' vast sections of the Norse sagas and could discuss 'with the best of them' the most efficient method of changing the chain on a Matchless motor bike.

Therefore, after having him thoroughly sprayed and fumigated by the county council, I decided to allow 'Doreen' (as we now called him) into my home.

I did not regret it, for during the course of his sojourn 'under my roof' he proved to be the most engaging of companions.

As a fixer of tap washers he had no peer.

As animal impersonator he put Percy Edwards completely 'in the shade'.

He was wittier by far than Tommy Handley.

He was brainier than Doctor Joad, braver than Monty and more beautiful than Jane.

Dear, dear 'Bath and' (as we now called him), he was indeed a Renaissance man – and he was still in short trousers.

And then the war ended and one day there was a knock on the front door of our house and we were confronted by a large red-faced woman, perspiring freely and snorting with rage through her hair-infested nostrils.

It was his mother.

She had come to collect him.

And so I saw dear 'Next-the-Sea' (as he had come to be known) being dragged tearfully down our front drive and disappearing in a cloud of dust into the 'vast unknown' beyond the confines of Witney Scrotum.

I sometimes wonder whatever became of him.

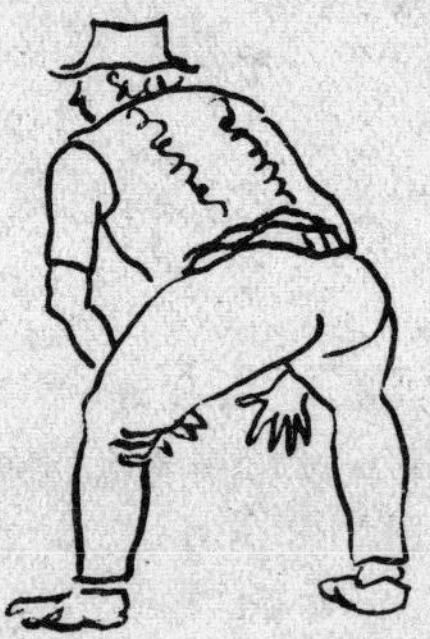

Mrs Shirley Williams:

What a splendid woman.

I bet her home's an absolute tip.

I bet it's a haven for everything a man could possibly desire in life – overflowing ashtrays, scuffed carpets, tide marks round the bath, dirty milk bottles on the table, stale clinkers in the fireplace, dust everywhere, countless back numbers of *The Cricketer* in the ablutions offices.

She'd let a man wear his socks in bed, no doubt about it.

She wouldn't talk during meal times.

She wouldn't mind if a chap smoked his pipe in the bath or stuck 'things' to the corner of the tablecloth.

She is everything a man could wish for in a woman.

Mr Henry Cooper:

He is the son of Lady Diana Cooper, from whom he learned much of his ringcraft and the whole of his diction.

I once saw him 'floor' Mr Bill 'Muhammed' Alley with a vicious left hook.

He holds the world record for 'heading the cricket ball'.

MR JOHN LENNON:

I confess I blubbed shamelessly when I heard the news of his death.

What wretchedness!
The world is indeed a woeful place.
I liked his music.
It was tip-top.

MR NEIL KINNOCK:

I dislike Welshmen intensely.

And I loathe and detest people with red hair.

Welshmen in my opinion (and I am not a prejudiced man) are all without exception whining, querulous, garrulous, joyless, mirthless, morose, malcontent, melancholic congenital tone-deaf hypochondriacs.

And as for men with red hair!

What I can't stand about them are their pink eyelids and their ghastly freckled noses and their thin little nostrils and the way they come up in blisters when they've been out in the sun and the way they're always bristling up to you and grabbing you by the lapels and trying to butt you in the nose and kick you in the nether regions of the popping crease.

Yes, Mr Kinnock will make an ideal leader of the Labour Party.

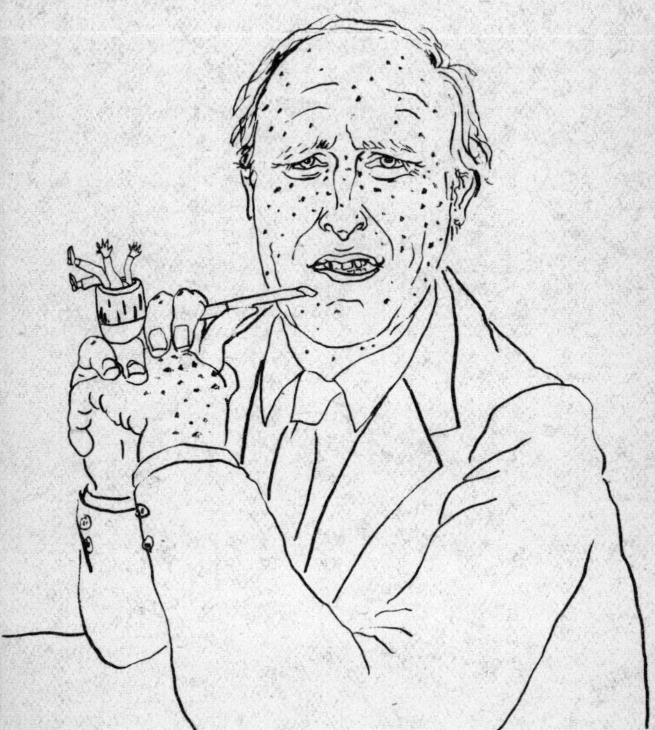

CAPTAIN MARK PHILLIPS:

Well, I ask you, is it any wonder?

Just look at the state of it.

Poor devil.

Still, imagine what you'd be like, dear readers, if you were married to that woman.

Mr Winston Place:

I have before me in my study at Witney Scrotum the estimable Mr Green's *Wisden Anthology, 1940–1963*.

I open the book at page 429, and what do I find?

I read as follows:

'E. Place bowled Dooland O.'

E. Place?

E.?

The man's name is Winston.

Winston. Winston. Winston, Mr Green.

For God's sake, Lennie, get his name right.

Dame Vera Lynn:

I do like the name Vera.

It has a 'homely' ring to it, doesn't it?

It is the sort of christian name borne by the wife of one's gardener.

The wife of our gardener at Witney Scrotum is called Hilary.

Hilary.

I find that most disturbing.

Hilary is the sort of christian name which should be borne by the wife of one's bank manager.

The wife of our bank manager at Witney Scrotum is called Sue.

Sue.

Dear God, everyone is called Sue these days.

Look at the names rolling up on the moving television screen.

All you see is Sue.

Sue, Sue, Sue.

What the hell is wrong with Vera?

If I had my way all these Sue creatures would be compelled to change their name by deed poll to Vera.

Vera Lawley – how pleasant.

Dame Vera Lawley is even better.

Much much better than Dame Sue Lynn.

I rest my case.

Mr Feliks Topolski:

I don't normally 'go for' foreigners, but I own to having had a soft spot for Feliks.

Under circumstances too complex to explain at this stage of the proceedings he was commissioned to paint a portrait of the lady wife.

When he delivered it to our house on his Rudge autocycle and unveiled it in our living room, the lady wife threw up her hands in horror.

'But it's nothing like me,' she said.

'I haven't got green skin.

'My eyes aren't purple.

'Both my arms are the same size, and as you well know I am not a hunchback with a goitre and a nose the shape and colour of a macaw's beak.

'It makes me look an absolute monster.'

The portrait now holds a place of honour on the wall of my study at Witney Scrotum.

MR ALAN AYCKBOURN:

Single-handedly this man has ruined more Scarborough cricket festivals than any creature, living, dead or in the curious 'twixt and tween' state of captaining Yorkshire County Cricket Club.

He is an out-and-out stinker.

And I have told him so.

In person.

Every year the lady wife insists on accompanying me to the festival and each evening drags me off to see one of his so-called plays, which apparently the wretch directs himself.

Well, he's got to, hasn't he?

No one else would be idiot enough to tackle it.

Good God, it's quite obvious to me that the stinker has never played cricket in his life.

The positions in which he places his actors on the stage are quite ludicrous.

There's never anyone on the boundary, and the slips are always hopelessly congested.

What a stinker.

My God, what an out-and-out stinker.

Sir John Hackett:

He is the much-loved 'second half' of the celebrated comedy duo, Minge and Hackett.

He is, I say without reservation, a man after my own heart.

I like the cut of his jib.

Splendid chap.

I'd be happy to make up a doubles at badminton with him any day of the week.

However, I am bound to say that I disagree wholeheartedly and profoundly with his philosophy of war.

In my opinion there is only one way for us to conduct our military affairs – let's go out immediately and make totally unprovoked war on the Dagos.

And while we're about it, we might as well knock the living daylights out of the Frogs and give the Nips a bloody good hiding.

What we have to do here in Britain is put these people 'in their place'.

I suggest that we all make a solemn vow here and now and go out tomorrow and cuff a Wop waiter round the earhole, lop off the right hand of an Arab shop-lifter and throw red paint over Mr Michael Heseltine.

That will make Britain 'Great' again, will it not?

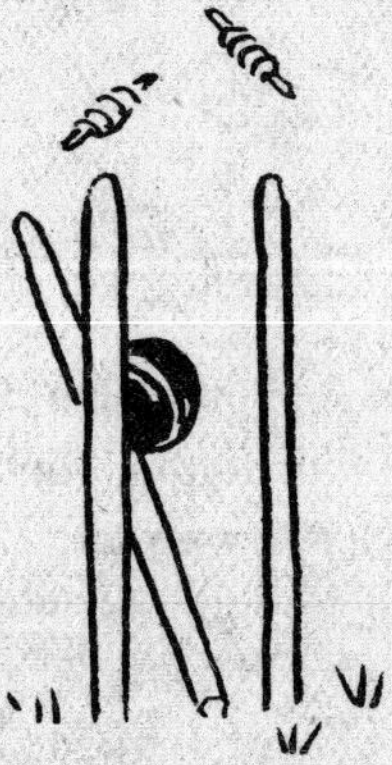